Forget

AMY LAURENS

OTHER WORKS

Forget

INKLET #39

AMY LAURENS

Inkprint
PRESS
www.inkprintpress.com

Print ISBN: 978-1-925825-38-1
eBook ISBN: 9781393001287

www.inkprintpress.com

National Library of Australia Cataloguing-in-Publication Data
Laurens, Amy 1985 –
Forget
42 p.
ISBN: 978-1-925825-38-1
Inkprint Press, Canberra, Australia
1. Fiction—Superheroes 2. Fiction—Short Stories

First Print Edition: August 2020
Cover image © Grae Dickason via Pixabay
Cover design © Inkprint Press
Interior art © Amy Laurens

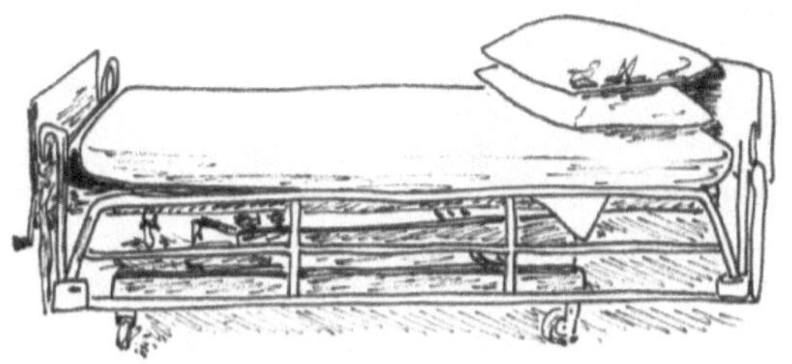

FORGET

He sits staring out the window, silent for the first time in weeks. They back out and close the door, taking their whisperings to the corridor.

If he could still feel, he'd be glad.

It is strange, this not-feeling. He can't remember ever being so tired. He can't remember...

No, that's just it.

He can't remember.

Remember what?

What?

Not all the memories are gone, of course. He knows that the building in which he now lives is some sort of aged care facility. He knows that the people who gather to whisper behind his closed door are mostly relatives, with a smattering of nursing staff and press.

He knows who he was, too. Simon Baker, 86, former proprietor of Deane, Baker & Sons.

But no. That's what he did, not who he was.

Who was he again?

He can't remember.

Remember?

What?

He is the last. I promise you, we are safe now. He cannot, will not, remember.
But what if he does?

He scratches idly at his temple, and feels as though he's chasing an idea that used to live there that now he can't recall.

Story of his life, these days.

The nurse comes in and deposits his lunch on the table, leaving without a word. It might be sad, if he could feel sad, but he is used to it: used to the silence they've locked him in, both inside and out.

No one talks to him now. They are polite, deferential—but silent.

And in his head, where he is quite sure there used to be thoughts—see, here, in his diary? He wrote things. He must have had these thoughts in order to write them down; but they are as foreign to him as the nurse who comes in every day, the one whose name he's sure he knows, but can't remember.

In his head, silence.
Can't remember.
Remember.
What?

And in this room is Mr Simon Baker, you may have heard of him, he's our most famous patient.

Is he sick?

No, little girl, he isn't sick. He's just old and fragile. There's nothing really wrong with him, but if we let him out he might hurt himself. He can't remember, you see.

Can't remember what?

Anything. He has... Alzheimer's, perhaps, or dementia. We're not quite sure.

That's sad.

It is a little—but he can't remember, you see, so he can't feel sad. So it's all okay.

Mum, look! This man can't remember.

Can't remember? What?

Outside the window a tree bends in the wind. It stirs a pleasant feeling in his chest, and he's struck with the nagging sensation that he used to know the word for this.

Once, when he was alive. Because he can't remember now, so he mustn't be alive. That's what he's decided, at any rate, and his diary agrees, so it must be true.

Even the nurse, when she delivers his food, is quieter, hardly daring to breathe in his presence.

He must be dead. Only the dead can't remember.

How's he doing?

Okay. I think. It's hard to know, he doesn't say anything.

But he's healthy?

Perfectly so. I saw the doctor yesterday; he says he's surprised at how well he's doing for someone his age.

You don't think it might be his po—

No. He can't remember a thing, remember? The mindwipe was complete. And it was his mind that controlled his body. If he can't remember, he can't think about it, and if he can't think about it he can't do it. No. We're safe.

Yes. I know. But is he?

The exhaustion seems to be deepening, even though physically he feels fine. It might even be strange, this feeling of his—but he can't remember what normal is, so maybe everything is normal. Maybe not remembering is normal. Maybe this cotton wool of living death is, after all, normal.

Maybe he never remembered.

Maybe he only dreamed of remembering.

Maybe no one remembers.

...and in major headlines, Simon Baker, last remaining Power, died in his nursing home today. While our hearts go out to his grieving family, all accounts agree that this was not unexpected. Rumours say that in his

last few months he contracted some form of brain degeneration, and his failing memory was the reason for the sudden loss of his powers.

Although any loss is tragic, I think we can all agree that we will sleep more soundly in our beds at night knowing that there are no longer any Powers left in the world.

He lay in the coffin, still. His heart beat so slowly it might as well have stopped; his mind moved glacially. But for all that, this was no worse than anything he remembered; and now he remembered. He remembered Powers clashing high in the sky, the ensuing storms destroying the earth below. He remembered War, with her flashing red eyes, and Peace, with eyes of mercy.

And he remembered himself:

Memory.

And he remembered all the pain and suffering that ever was, all the hardships that ever will be. And he knew that some things are best forgotten.

In the end, we can't actually remember what happened. One day the world was fine, and the next... Well, it was all a mess, and it's all sort of a blur. We—none of us—can't really recall.

But it's a devastating war, one that's wiped out three quarters of Earth's population. Doesn't anyone know why it began?

That's just the thing. No one can remember.

Remember?

What?

THE MAKING OF
FORGET

This little story was part of the first cluster of short stories I sold back in the second half of 2010. I'd spent three years hanging out on Critique Circle, making writing friends while doing a couple of university courses on creative writing, trying hard to learn how to write short stories in particular as well as stories generally.

During that time, I'd also done my teaching qualifications. During my final prac, I had the chance to work with one of my university professors who somehow was also still teaching a line of high school English. One of his students was working a project that speculated on the connection between death and memory, and that intrigued me. What if the opposite of death wasn't life, but memory instead? What if we only died when we were forgotten, and only lived while we were remembered?

Around the same time, I decided I wanted to write something about superheroes, preferably set in opposing pairs—so of course, one was going to be Death, and their opposite was going to be Memory.

But what happened when Death came for Memory?

When Memory himself began to forget?

And thus, the story was born.

DOWNLOAD YOUR FREE EBOOK

When you buy a print book from Inkprint Press, we like to say THANK YOU by offering you the ebook for free!

Please head to www.inkprintpress.com/inklets/39/ and the use the coupon 39INK to get your copy of this Inklet in epub AND mobi today!
(Coupon will only work once.)

Read more by Amy Laurens!

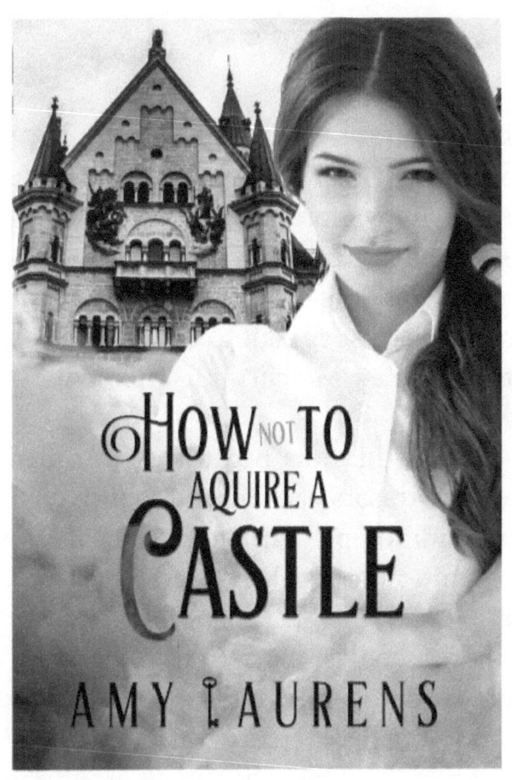

HOW NOT TO ACQUIRE A CASTLE

CHAPTER ONE

ON A HARD PLASTIC CHAIR IN THE FRONT row of the Great Hall in the world's fifth-best evil overlording academy, with its red-wooden parquetry floor that spoke of wealth and the beige, square panels of sound-boards speaking of conservatism on the walls, Mercury sat, pointedly not sweating.

Partly, this was because the Academy Administrators had deigned to turn on the air-conditioning earlier in the day, in recognition of the fact that the hall would be packed out with approximately six hundred bodies, all here to celebrate the graduation of about a third of that crowd.

But mostly, Mercury was pointedly not sweating because she made it a point never to sweat, sweat being an indication that she was working hard, and hard work being antithetical to her way of life.

However. If she *had* been sweating right now, it would not have been due to the uncomfortable warmth of six hundred packed bodies that even the air-conditioning system couldn't completely shift, or, in fact, from overexertion. Instead, it would have been caused by an even more unfamiliar concept in Mercury's emotional vocabulary: nervousness.

Mercury did not *get* nervous. Mercury got things *done*.

So the fact that she was sitting here, in the front row of the Great Hall, about to graduate from Evil Overlording Academy (with distinction), and was feeling *nervous*... She crumpled the black paper program in her pale fists. It made her furious, that's what it did.

Abjectly furious, that snooty-tooty Deviran with his stupid morals and his stupid I-don't-want-to-be-here and his stupid Overlords-are-empty-figureheads and his stupid face sitting ten people over, looking implacable with his deep brown skin and barely-there, precision-groomed beard, as though he knew it gave him a stupid air of alluringly stupid mystery…

Mercury scowled and searched for the train of thought that had been derailed, yet again, by Deviran's stupidity.

Ah. Yes. She was angry because she was nervous because she wasn't absolutely entirely one hundred and fifty percent sure that she'd beaten Deviran in their final exams, and 1) being anything less than a hundred and fifty percent certain of anything made her cranky, and 2) being beaten by Deviran for dux of the year would be utterly unbearable. She flicked away a piece of fluff that had become snagged under her immaculately magenta-painted nails and smoothed out the black paper program.

In the front corner of the hall, the starkly-attired string quartet with their traditional black instruments began playing the March of the Oncoming Doom. The screechy scrapes of hundreds of chairs on the hall's wooden floor sounded as the crowd climbed to its collective feet.

Mercury sat with her arms firmly folded for a few moments longer, until her best friend Sparky kicked her in the ankle.

"Get up, idiot," Sparky hissed, hints of real flame flickering through her flame-coloured pixie cut.

"No," Mercury said, flouncing to her feet and tossing her own glossy brown hair back over her shoulders. Four years she'd been playing by the Academy's rules in order to get what she wanted, and she'd had just about enough. Other people's rules should only be applied to plebs too stupid to invent their own.

Sparky rolled her eyes somewhere over Mercury's head before focusing on the stage, where the ceremonial party had begun entering.

Mercury clenched her jaw and narrowed her own eyes as the teachers of the Evil Overlording Academy filed onto the stage, dressed in their formal finery. Each teacher had their own distinctive look that matched their personality and their Overlording style, from severe charcoal suits to jet-black leathers, pastel ball-gowns and gem-toned lingerie and eye-blinding spandex, and even on one tiny old woman at the back, worn jeans and a grey flannel shirt. She was the one to watch out for, of course; Mercury could respect an Overlord who was confident enough in their abilities that they didn't need to telegraph them. It wasn't a look *she* would consider, of course, but still. She could respect it.

The band's march finished and, after a moderately awkward pause, the crowd sat. The Principal, pale skin and dark hair matching his suspiciously vampiric red-and-black suit, took the podium, and Mercury narrowed her eyes. He was doing a superb job of hiding his emotions—he was a premier Evil Overlord, after all—but she was Mercury, and unlike anyone else, she had the benefit of being able to rummage through people's consciousnesses. She was better at adding things *into* people's minds than taking information out, but he was telegraphing fear loudly enough that she could sense it without trying overly much.

Mercury pursed her lips.
Hmm.

The Principal cleared his throat at the blackened-wood podium, and the fear made it into his usually-unreadable eyes. "Before we begin," he said, and Mercury's stomach did a peculiar kind of flip-flop. "I have a pressing announcement to make regarding the safety of our students and their families."

He cleared his throat again and took out a sheet of paper from his pocket, unfolding it carefully and smoothing out the creases before beginning again. "The Council"—quiet booing echoed around the hall, and Mercury tsked impatiently— "have asked me to recommend that students from Tumul Tuos seriously consider postponing their return to town for a few days. The city is dealing with a *situation* at present which may present a danger to our students' health and safety."

Mercury's hands fisted at her sides and she forced herself to remain seated. What was wrong with her city? What had the Council mucked up now? A risk to the students' safety? There had to be more he wasn't telling them. Gently, Mercury tugged on his consciousness, implanting the suggestion that it might be better to share the news than to keep it secret. After all, how could they fight an enemy they didn't know?

"There are, ah…" He trailed off, glancing side to side as though wondering why his mouth had decided to continue.

Mercury didn't snicker, but she did press her lips together in satisfaction.

The Principal took a deep, steadying breath and seemed to change tack. "There has been one death already. The family have already been notified, so it is with much regret that I must inform you that Woovermyer will no longer be with us at the Evil Overlording Academy."

Murmurs broke out around the room, not all of them sad—to be expected in a school devoted to raising the next generation of dictators (ish) and despots (of sorts).

Mercury, however, crushed her program in her left hand, fist so tight her nails bit her palm.

"You okay?" Sparky murmured, leaning towards her.

Mercury gave a single, tense shake of her head and stared at the podium. Dead. Livie Woovermyer was dead in *her city*. And the Council hadn't done anything to stop it. Couldn't do anything to stop it, probably, given they'd warned the students to stay away. Livie hadn't been the strongest candidate in the year level, but she was no lightweight, either. It would take a lot of power to kill a Seven.

Enough was enough. A good thing Mercury was about to graduate at the top of the class, giving her the right to knock the lowest ranking current Overlord off their perch. Tumul Tuos would be hers in a matter of hours. And then there'd be no more of these wasteful deaths. Her city would be safe at last.

Madame Pompadour was up the front now, elbow gloves the same glimmery silver colour as her elaborate, piled-curls wig, eyelids gleaming with matching silver eye shadow, and abruptly Mercury realised Madame was there to make the announcement that would change her life forever. She leaned forward in her seat, ready to stand when her name was called.

"And now the announcement you've all been dying for," the Political Alliances teacher trilled, the frills on her evening gown fluttering as she moved. "The dux of this year's cohort!"

Sweat slicked Mercury's palms. Irritated, she reached over and wiped them on Sparky's thigh.

Sparky pushed Mercury's hands back into her own personal space bubble and Mercury, nervous to the edge of distraction, let her.

"Will you please join me in welcoming to the stage, our wonderful dux for this year, Deviran Goodsmith!"

Mercury froze halfway to standing. "Did she just say Deviran?" she whispered furiously to Sparky.

Sparky hauled her forcibly back down into her seat. "Yes," she hissed back. "Sit down, you're making a fool of yourself."

Mercury's spine snapped upright as she sat, and she arranged the folds of her long black skirt demurely. "No I'm not." She closed her eyes. "Deviran's going up to the stage, isn't he?" Even at a whisper, the misery in her voice was clear, but this time, she didn't care.

Sparky reached over and squeezed her hand.

Mercury squeezed back, lacing her fingers through Sparky's, and held tight as all her plans and dreams vanished in front of her.

A stone had landed in her chest. That must be it. Some strange sort of magic that made her chest contract and sink, and made the world distort for just a moment, long enough to trick her into thinking Deviran had beaten her so that someone could jump in front of her and yell SURPRISE!

Any moment now.

Any moment.

She refused to open her eyes and watch Deviran parading across the stupid stage like some stupid stupid-person, receiving his stupid medal and stupid symbolic crest pin.

It was that last exam question. She'd known Deviran would pull out his ridiculous 'Evil Overlords are merely figureheads, the Business Guild is where the power really lies' rant that everyone had heard a million times back when he was younger and angrier, and she'd tried to counter it, she really had.

She'd argued for the importance of the Overlording position, for the power of having a symbolic figure to unite the population in their hatred, for having a person able to make all the difficult, necessary decisions the Council was too weak and spineless to make... But it hadn't been enough. Everything she'd worked for, everything she'd set out to prove—and it wasn't enough.

There were words, there were names, and then forever later, once she'd died twice already, Sparky elbowed her in the ribs. "Come on," Sparky muttered. "We're up next."

And sure enough, there was a shuffling of presenters as the last of the Powers Behind The Thone graduates departed the stage, and the next speaker announced in threatening, funereal tones, "The Overlording cohort."

Mercury blinked furiously and followed Sparky to the end of the line at the right side of the stage. The other candidates proceeded one at a time across the stage, two girls and then stupid Deviran, and then a handful more and then Sparky, and then the speaker was calling her name.

Hands fisted, Mercury tossed her head high, climbed the four steps, and marched across the stage. She wouldn't look at them, the stupid faculty who'd denied her the city she rightfully deserved, and she wouldn't look the other way either, at the classmates and crowd undoubtedly sniggering at her failure.

She shook hands with the presenter, and while he pinned the tiny crossedswords badge on her collar, her eyes betrayed her and slid towards the audience. Her stomach flipped as she saw the crowd of parents and friends behind the rows of students, all the way to the back of the hall, twenty rows at least, illuminated by the late afternoon light streaming in through the ceiling-high windows to the right. Everyone had someone here to watch them graduate. Everyone except Weird Al—and her.

The presenter finished with her pin, muttered something to her, and offered his hand again. Mercury coldly ignored it and strode from the stage. It didn't matter. None of it mattered. Tumul Tuos was her city anyway, and no one could change that. She'd think of something. She'd take a day or two out, make some plans...

And she could always hope that Deviran would choose some other Overlording territory. He'd be stupid to, but then again, he was stupid, so. Mercury could hope.

All at once, mid-way down the steps off the stage, Mercury came to rigid attention, scanning the room. Somewhere out there in the crowd, an exchange of power had just taken place, and it felt... unusual.

But the final few students were backing up behind her and muttering, so Mercury headed back toward her seat, craning her head all the while and searching for some sign of whatever it was that had just discharged a dizzyingly quiet amount of power into the room.

She sat, and Sparky leaned over. "Okay?"

"Mm," said Mercury. "Did you feel…" She accidentally caught the eye of the student behind her and twisted back to face the front.

"Feel what?"

Mercury turned it over in her mind. It had felt like a large shot of power discharged very quietly—but perhaps it hadn't been. Perhaps it had only been a small discharge after all, something most people wouldn't have noticed.

But still, something about it had tugged on her. It very nearly felt like something she'd felt before, only she *knew* she'd never sensed that kind of discharge before.

She shook her head. "Never mind. Don't worry."

Sparky sighed and straightened. "It's fine, Mercury," she said, drily exasperated.

"I know you didn't win, but I promise, you'll live through it."

Mercury waved a hand for silence.

The power had just discharged again, and it had come from somewhere in the back corner, far away from the windows and light.

Impatiently, Mercury waited for the formalities to conclude. The crowd stood while the quartet played the exit march, and the stage party left, Mercury tapping her foot all the while.

The moment the last notes of the march died away, Mercury turned and headed to the back corner, weaving in and out of the students and parents who had seemed to explode slowly but inexorably out from the neat rows of seating, ignoring Sparky's calls behind her. Power, something that tugged in a way that was strange and familiar, all at once. She pushed her way through a family posing for pictures—and halted.

In the shadows of the back corner, Deviran stood with his family, with his stupid, smug little smile, looking as tall and dark and stupidly alluring as ever. Prat.

His mother, short but sleek, and his father—tall, and utterly terrifying in a way not at all diminished by his gleaming smile—gushed over him, patting his back and hugging him tight. Within moments the Principal was there, glibly shaking hands and congratulating them on the success of their son. Something flickered across his consciousness, and also Deviran's father's—some moment of recognition in response to what they were saying.

But Mercury brushed it aside just as the mother brushed melodramatic tears from her cheeks and handed Deviran a silver-wrapped package about as long as her hand but half the width.

That. That was the source of the strange, magical feeling. Mercury watched hawk-eyed as Deviran un-wrapped the gift. A glimpse of gold set her pulse racing—What was it? What did it do? Could she steal it?—and then the paper fell away to the floor, and Deviran stood staring wordlessly at the object in his hands, and Mercury did too.

Wide-eyed, Deviran raised his gaze to his parents, and even from where she stood Mercury could hear the reverence in his voice as he thanked them.

But Mercury had eyes only for the object. No wonder she'd felt it discharge, and no wonder it had felt both strange and familiar. In Deviran's hands lay a glorious, sunshine-gold key, large and strong—and with a handle in the shape of a stylised fish, long, flowing fins curving to make the grip.

A Key. They'd given him a Key. And not just any Key, but *the* Key, *her* Key, the Artefact of Power belonging to *her* city.

A wordless noise of wanting rose in Mercury's throat. Who cared about being dux? She needed that Key.

Keep reading! Head to
www.amylaurens.com/books/
kaditeos/castle
to buy your copy now!

AMY LAURENS is an Australian author of fantasy fiction for all ages.

In addition to the *Inklet* short stories, Amy has also written the award-winning portal-fantasy *Sanctuary* series about Edge, a 13-year-old girl forced to move to a small country town because of witness protection (the first book is *Where Shadows Rise*), the humorous fantasy *Kaditeos* series, following newly graduated Evil Overlord Mercury as she attempts to acquire a castle, the young adult series *Storm Foxes*, about love and magic and mental health, and a whole host of non-fiction.

INKLETS

Collect them all! Released on the 1st and 15th
of each month.

INKLET #031
Welcome to Dark Dale
LIANA BROOKS

INKLET #032
When War Came to Town
A Powers Story
AMY LAURENS

INKLET #033
Not Fantasy
AMY LAURENS

INKLET #034
Courting the Winter Prince
LIANA BROOKS

INKLET #035
At the Home of the Winter King
A Winter Powers Story
AMY LAURENS

INKLET #036
With This Ring
AMY LAURENS

INKLET #037
Venus &
Seven Reasons I Said No
LIANA BROOKS

INKLET #038
OATH KEEPER
AMY LAURENS

INKLET #039
FORGET
A Powers Story
AMY LAURENS

INKLET #040
NOT QUITE Cinderella
LIANA BROOKS

INKLET #041
ONE BAD MAN
AMY LAURENS

DOUBLE ISSUE
INKLET #042
The Claustrophobia Of Loneliness &
Adam, Be A Star
AMY LAURENS

INKLET #043
The Artist as a Young Girl
LIANA BROOKS

INKLET #044
CONFESSIONS
AMY LAURENS

INKLET #045
But For Snow
A Kaditeos Story
AMY LAURENS

INKLET #046
The Boy Named NO
LIANA BROOKS

INKLET #047
Anamata
AMY LAURENS

INKLET #048
A Wolf FOR Christmas
AMY LAURENS